Classic — BEDTIME STORIES

Classic
BEDTIME STORIES

Illustrated by SCOTT GUSTAFSON

GREENWICH WORKSHOP PRESS

In loving memory of my dad, Maynard Gustafson.

I WOULD LIKE TO THANK *the friends and family members who good-naturedly served as models for some of the characters in this book: Cortney Conrad, Patty and Karl Gustafson, the Mariselvam family, Corie Sparlin, Lisa Stran, and Griffin White. Also, I send my thanks and appreciation to Mary Coriglione, who, as always, is there to help a friend in need; to Wendy Wentworth, for her sound judgment and tireless work behind the scenes; to Scott Usher, for his seemingly endless ability to take negatives and turn them into positives. And a special thanks to my wife, Patty, for her much-needed technical support, love and enduring faith. S.G.*

 A GREENWICH WORKSHOP PRESS BOOK
Copyright ©2014 The Greenwich Workshop Press
All art ©2014 Scott Gustafson. All rights reserved.
All text ©2014 Scott Gustafson (with the exception of
The Story of Little Sambha and the Tigers).
www.scottgustafson.com

Published by The Greenwich Workshop, Inc.
151 Main St., Seymour, CT 06483
(800) 243-4246

Fine art prints of Scott Gustafson's paintings are available through The Greenwich Workshop, Inc. www.greenwichworkshop.com

Jacket front: *Jack and the Beanstalk*
Jacket back: *The King and Queen and Briar Rose*

Design: Bjorn Akselsen
Photography: Bob Hixon

ISBN 978-0-86713-158-1
Manufactured in China by Oceanic Graphic Printing
Second Printing 2014
2 3 4   17 16 15 14

CONTENTS

The Country Mouse
AND THE CITY MOUSE

ONCE THERE WERE TWO MICE that had been playmates when they were young but life had taken them on different paths, and they had gone their separate ways. One lived in the country whereas the other had chosen to live in the city.

Then one day, by chance, their paths crossed again.

Right then and there, they decided to renew their old friendship.

"You should come for a visit to the country," said the country mouse. "The fresh air will do you good."

"That does sound splendid," agreed the city mouse. "How does the day after tomorrow sound?"

So it was that the date and the time were set and the country mouse hurried home that very day and began to get ready for his visitor.

He loved the quiet little corner of the old barn that he called home. The farmer's granary and corncrib offered food in a never-ending supply, and for variety there were seeds in the garden and nut trees in the yard. Beyond that, the rolling fields and lush meadows offered the most beautiful views.

He spent the rest of the day tidying up and gathering the finest foods he could find. At last, everything was ready, and the country mouse couldn't wait to share his lovely home with his old friend.

Early the next morning, the city mouse arrived and from the start, things didn't go well. He was dusty from the journey and the country breeze had mussed up his fancy hair, but he made the best of it and smiled faintly as the excited country mouse showed him around. It wasn't long, however, before the country mouse was seeing his humble home through the sophisticated eyes of the city mouse. And by the time they sat down to lunch, the poor country mouse was feeling that his rustic lifestyle really wasn't that much to be proud of after all.

"You really must come to the city," sniffed the city mouse, as he politely nibbled at a dried bean. "The food alone is to die for." He returned the barely touched bean to his plate and declared he simply could not eat another bite.

So first thing the next morning, they set out for town. Once inside the city limits, it was now the city mouse that grew excited and happily pointed out all the cultural attractions and features of interest. Compared to the country, the city certainly did have a lot going on. Then, in front of a grand house on a beautiful, cobblestoned street, the city mouse suddenly stopped.

"Well, this is it. Home, Sweet Home!" he smiled proudly.

Inside, they toured room after room, each more lovely than the last. They scampered across fine carpets and strolled beneath richly polished furniture. Finally, they came into the dining room.

"Ah, we're in luck," beamed the city mouse. "The Master of the house is preparing for a party!"

Within moments, they climbed onto the table and were surrounded by the most glorious array of food that the country mouse had ever seen. Cakes, pies, roast meats, breads, exotic fruits and more were all displayed on silver platters and crystal glassware.

They had just begun to nibble at a delicious cake when one of the servants came bustling into the room to rearrange the flowers. Quickly, the two mice hid behind a silver coffee pot. Again and again, just as they thought the coast was clear and that they could enjoy some of the bounty, yet another human would enter the room, making the two mice hide in fear. Soon, the candles were lit and the guests began to arrive, and with them went all hope of ever having a moment's peace.

As the two mice escaped from the dining room and into a cramped, dark hole in the wall that the city mouse called his "bedchamber," the country mouse made a decision.

"You know, old friend," he said, "You are surrounded by the finest food and furnishings that money can buy, but you can't enjoy any of it. To you, my food and home may be simple, but I now realize that it's the simple life for me!"

With that, the old friends shook hands and once more parted ways. The country mouse returned to the country and the city mouse remained in town. Each mouse remained in his own home, happy with the life he had chosen.

SLEEPING *Beauty*

MANY YEARS AGO there was a King and Queen who, more than anything, wanted to have a child. Years went by and still there was no baby for the royal couple. Then one morning, while the Queen bathed in the pool in her private garden, an old frog poked its head out of the water. He told her that soon she would indeed give birth to the long awaited heir. Within months, a lovely little girl was born and because she was so delicate and beautiful they named the princess Briar Rose.

Overjoyed by this wonderful event, the King and Queen wanted to share their happiness and declared that a feast in honor of their new daughter would be given. Among the many invited guests were twelve fairies that lived in the Kingdom. There was a thirteenth fairy, but no one had seen her outside of her tower for over fifty years, and everyone assumed that she was either dead or bewitched. So the King, hoping to ensure the favor of the other twelve fairies ordered the royal goldsmith to create twelve golden place settings. These included beautifully made plates, goblets, knives, forks and spoons, all encrusted with precious gems and laid especially at the places where each fairy was to sit.

Finally, the feast day came and all of the guests, including the twelve fairies had been seated when, much to the embarrassment of the royal hosts, an uninvited guest arrived. It was the thirteenth fairy, and she was angry that she had not received an invitation.

Hurriedly, a chair was found and a place was set, but this did little to sweeten the fairy's sour mood. Then, when she saw that her place setting was the same china, crystal and silverware as the other guests and not made of gold and jewels like those of the other, younger, fairies, she became enraged and muttered curses and vile oaths under her breath. She barely touched the sumptuous meal that was set before her.

Fortunately, the youngest fairy, who was seated nearby, saw all of this and while the third course was being served, she slipped, unnoticed, from the table and hid behind a heavy curtain that hung in the dining hall.

As was the custom in that land, after the feast had been served, the guests stepped forward to bring presents to the new Princess. But the fairies brought more than material gifts. They brought gifts no one could hold in their hands. The first fairy gave the child the gift of inner beauty, the second, intelligence, the third, the patience of a saint, the fourth, gracefulness, and so on. When the eleventh fairy had finished granting Briar Rose the gift of an angelic singing voice, the old fairy rose from her chair. Trembling with rage and shaking her fist at the innocent child, she hissed.

"Before the dawn of her fifteenth birthday, this Princess shall prick her finger on the spindle of a spinning wheel and die!"

And with that, she stormed out of the hall, leaving the royal parents and all of the guests gasping at the cruelty of the curse. But before the King and Queen could shed a single tear, the youngest fairy, who had feared something like this might happen, stepped out from behind the curtain where she had been hiding.

"Don't be afraid!" her young voice rose strong and clear above the cries and murmurs. "There is still one gift yet to be given, and even though I cannot undo what has been done, I do believe I can soften it." Turning to the cradle she spoke gently, "Princess, you shall prick your finger on the spindle of a spinning wheel, but instead of dying, you will fall into a deep sleep that will last for one hundred years, after which, you will be awakened by a brave and noble Prince."

The King, in an attempt to avoid the prophecy, made a royal proclamation that all the spinning wheels and spindles within the castle and kingdom were to be destroyed. Anyone disobeying this law would be executed.

For almost fifteen years, the King's law seemed to work. Briar Rose grew from an adorable baby into a poised and beautiful Princess, and in time everyone forgot about the curse. Then, within a week of her fifteenth birthday, the King and Queen were called away on business to one of their distant palaces. Left alone in the castle, the Princess felt the urge to explore. It was funny, she thought, that even though she had spent her whole life in this castle, there were still rooms and passages that she had yet to discover. Days were spent running up stairs and down corridors, and there were storerooms, empty chambers and musty attics that were all new to her.

At last, she entered an old tower, and at the top of a winding stone stairway she found a door with a rusty key in its ancient lock. As she turned it, the door swung open onto a little room in which a very old woman was hunched over a strange device. The thing hummed and whirred while the woman sang softly to herself. Briar Rose was intrigued. She had never seen anything like it before.

"What are you doing?" the girl asked innocently.

"Spinning, my beauty. Spinning!" the old woman replied.

"May I try?" the Princess asked.

"Certainly!" The old creature couldn't help but smile at the girl's eagerness and motioned her to come closer. "Just put your hands here…"

No sooner had Briar Rose touched the spinning wheel, than her finger was pricked on the sharp spindle. Before she could draw another breath, the Princess fell to the floor in a swoon.

If it hadn't been for the sound of an old woman's cackle, the palace guard might never have noticed that the old tower door had been left open. There, in a room at the top of the stairs, lying alone on the floor as if dead, he found the Princess. Chambermaids, butlers and royal ministers all ran to see if they could help the girl. The court doctors were summoned and they tried every known remedy, but nothing would revive her. They would have feared that she was dead, except for the soft blush of her cheeks, the lovely red lips and the gentle rise and fall of her breast that told them that Briar Rose was merely asleep.

A court messenger was sent to bring the terrible news to the King and Queen, and they raced homeward in a speeding carriage drawn by the fastest horses in the realm.

The court doctors had the Princess moved to her own bed, and her maids dressed her in the loveliest of gowns. And when, at last, the girl's parents arrived home and rushed immediately to her chamber, that is how they found her.

The news spread quickly through the fairy realm until it reached the young fairy herself. Within moments she too arrived at the castle. She approved of all that had been done for the Princess but soon realized a troubling fact. When, in a hundred years, Briar Rose did awaken, none of her family, friends or courtiers would still be alive to greet her, and she would be surrounded by strangers. It was then that the fairy decided that everyone in the castle should sleep for as long as their Princess slept. Tapping each person with her magic wand, she sent them into a deep sleep.

Everyone, no matter whom or where, fell under the silent enchantment. Ministers arguing over matters of state drifted off in mid-sentence. Ladies-in-waiting waited in slumber while the knife in the hand of the scullery maid quietly ceased to peel. Down in the royal kennel, the stable boy napped with the hounds while high on the battlements the guards drifted into peaceful sleep. Even a castle gargoyle struggled to stifle a stony yawn.

Once everyone else in the castle was fast asleep, the fairy told the King and Queen her plan. After kissing Briar Rose goodnight, the royal couple seated themselves on their thrones and then, they too, were tapped by the magic wand and fell into a deep, deep sleep.

In order to protect and shield them from the prying eyes of the outside world, the fairy immediately caused great thorn bushes to grow up and surround the castle. Thick branches studded with razor sharp barbs wrapped themselves about the walls and grew up over the battlements until only the tallest weather-vane on top of the highest tower remained uncovered. In time, this too would become enveloped in the ever-thickening growth.

So, in stillness, the quiet castle waited for the next hundred years. Cloaked in a shroud of dense, green briar, it silently cradled the sleeping Princess whose beauty rivaled that of the freshly blooming rose.

It came to pass that in the hundredth year of the enchantment, the son of a nearby king was hunting in the forest surrounding the bewitched castle. From afar, the Prince could make out what appeared to be the outline of roofs and towers beneath the dense foliage and thorns. He asked the other

members of his hunting party if they knew the story behind this mysterious place, but no one could help him. Finally, an old peasant who lived in those parts came forward, removed his hat, bowed and said,

"Your highness, over sixty years ago when I was just a boy, my father told me that within those walls lies a beautiful Princess, the most lovely Princess anyone has ever seen. It was her curse that she was to sleep there for a hundred years until awakened by the son of a king, whose arrival she awaits."

Without a single doubt, the Prince believed that he must truly be that pre-destined son of a king that the old man spoke of. Drawing his sword, the Prince advanced upon the thorny thicket. He intended to chop his way through every inch of the dense undergrowth if need be.

But, to his amazement, the thick branches drew back, revealing an easily traveled corridor before him. Stepping a few paces down that path, the thorns he passed transformed themselves into blooming roses. But when he turned to call back to his friends, the thorn bushes grew up behind him again, thicker than before, allowing none of the others to come after him. But being a brave young fellow, he decided to continue on alone.

That bravery, however, was soon tested — for entangled in the thorny thicket on either side he could see the skeletons of men, dressed in ancient armor and clutching rusty swords in their bony hands. Truly, these were men who had come before, others who had heard the story and thought that they, too, were destined for the sleeping Princess. But still, the Prince pressed on and still the thorns yielded before him. Eventually, a wide avenue of trees opened up, at the end of which could easily be seen the castle gates. As he drew nearer, his heart stopped when he saw what appeared to be more fallen suitors lying in the courtyard ahead. But when he reached them, he found that they were the palace guards fast asleep, for their cheeks were rosy and some of them even snored.

Others must have been drinking when sleep came upon them, for in their hands they still held cups half-filled with wine.

He stepped over sleeping guards and entered the castle. He continued past a scrubber woman who, in mid-scrub, now slept on the soapy stairs. Every hallway and apartment seemed to hold someone who had fallen asleep while performing their duties; servants with trays were sprawled on carpets, wise counselors debating and elegant ladies-in-waiting were slumped in silent slumber. As he went past the throne room he saw courtiers dozing and the King and Queen sleeping in their royal chairs. Even the fires in the palace fireplaces seemed to snooze in flameless repose.

Finally, up past the grand staircase, through a maze of chambers and ante-chambers and down a long corridor, the Prince at last came to an elegant door. Delicately carved on the door was the name, Briar Rose. His heart pounded as he lifted the latch and went in.

Sunlight filtering through the vine-covered windows dappled across the royal bed, and his heart stopped as he drew back the heavy curtains. He forgot to breathe — she truly was the most beautiful princess that he had ever seen!

Whether he kissed her then or not, we shall never know, for no one was there to see, and the Princess would never tell. But whatever happened, one thing was sure: the final hour of the final year of the long enchantment had, at that moment, come to an end, and as destiny would have it, her eyelids fluttered and she awoke.

Then, she looked at him, not in surprise or embarrassment, but with tenderness.

"Is that you, my Prince?" she asked. "I have waited for you for such a long time!"

He fell in love with her at that very instant, and as he sat down on the bed beside her, the two began talking together like people who had known each other all their lives. The air about them was alive with happiness and excitement, and they could have talked like that for hours. The only note of discontent was struck by Chloe, the Princess' pet kitten, who was jealous to awaken and find the Prince getting more attention than she.

By this time, the enchantment had lifted from the rest of the castle, and everyone stretched and yawned, then continued on with whatever they had been doing one hundred years ago. The scullery maid proceeded to pluck the feathers from the fowl due to be roasted, while the cook scolded a page for spilling the Queen's tea tray.

Of all those awakening in the castle that day, only the King and Queen knew that they too had been enchanted. Once awake, they hurried to see their daughter. The last time they had seen the Princess, she was deep in a deathlike sleep. Now, when they reached her chamber door, they heard two excited voices and laughter coming from within. Upon opening the door, they were delighted to find their daughter dancing around the room with a handsome prince, as she announced that the two of them were engaged to be married.

Overjoyed, the King and Queen proclaimed that the wedding feast would happen that very day. The whole castle rejoiced, not only for the happy couple, but for the feast as well. After all, it had been a hundred years since any of them had eaten and they had all grown quite hungry!

Already dressed in her most stunning gown, the Princess made a lovely bride. After the vows were exchanged, the party began. The bride was indeed breathtaking, and the groom obviously adored her, and everyone agreed that they had never seen a happier couple.

As the feast continued late into the night, the Prince did, at times, feel like he was stepping back in time. The hundred-year-old music played by the Court's musicians sounded ancient and the conversations of many of the dinner guests were absolutely historic. But none of that really mattered to the young couple. To them, their love was the love of the century. And the truly magical thing was, they felt that way for the rest of their lives.

THE TORTOISE
and the Hare

ONE DAY A HARE was making fun of a tortoise for being slow, while at the same time he bragged about his own speed.

"I'll race you," the tortoise said quietly.

"You'll WHAT?!" the hare laughed.

"I said, I'll race you," the tortoise repeated.

"HA! You race me? That's a laugh!" the hare guffawed. "Why, I'd be at the finish line before you even got started!"

"And I bet I'll win," the tortoise calmly continued.

"It's a bet!" cried the hare, and the two shook hands on the wager.

They asked a fox to judge the race and set the finish line, and then they were off. With amazing speed, the hare was away and rounding the first bend before the tortoise had taken even a few steps. Soon, the hare had run so far ahead that he could no longer even see the tortoise behind him.

"Maybe I'll just wait here until I can actually see the fleet-footed Mr. Tortoise," the hare chuckled, as he stretched in the shade of a roadside tree. "And to think that tortoise bet that he could beat me!" The smirking hare leaned back against the tree and closed his eyes. "What a chump!" Soon he was fast asleep.

Meanwhile, the tortoise kept right on steadily putting one foot in front of the other as he slowly plodded along. He even plodded on tiptoe as he passed the tree where the hare blissfully dozed.

The hare had no idea when, exactly, the tortoise had passed him. In fact, it wasn't until sometime much later that he finally woke up. But by then it was too late. Even though he ran with all of his might, the hare reached the finish line just in time to see the tortoise cross it before him.

The moral of the story is, "slow and steady, wins the race!"

THE STORY OF
 *Little Sambha and the Tigers*

ONCE UPON A TIME there was a young boy, and his name
was Little Sambha.

And his mother was called Maata.

And his father was called Baapa.

One day Maata made him a beautiful little red coat, and a pair of beautiful
little blue trousers.

And Baapa went to the bazaar, and bought him a beautiful green umbrella,
and a lovely little pair of purple shoes with crimson soles and crimson linings.

And then wasn't Little Sambha grand?

So he put on all his fine clothes, and went out for a walk in the jungle. By and by, he met a tiger and the tiger said to him, "Little Sambha, I'm going to eat you up!"

And Little Sambha said, "Oh! Please, Mr. Tiger, don't eat me up, and I'll give you my beautiful little red coat."

So the tiger said, "Very well, I won't eat you this time, but you must give me your beautiful little red coat." So the tiger got poor Little Sambha's beautiful little red coat, and went away saying, "Now I'm the grandest tiger in the jungle."

And Little Sambha walked on and by and by he met another tiger, and he said to him, "Little Sambha, I'm going to eat you up!" And Little Sambha said, "Oh! Please, Mr. Tiger, don't eat me up, and I'll give you my beautiful little blue trousers." So the tiger got poor Little Sambha's beautiful little blue trousers, and went away saying, "Now I'm the grandest tiger in the jungle."

And Little Sambha went on and by and by he met another tiger, and it said to him, "Little Sambha, I'm going to eat you up!" And Little Sambha said, "Oh! Please, Mr. Tiger, don't eat me up, and I'll give you my beautiful little purple shoes with crimson soles and crimson linings."

But the tiger said, "What use would your shoes be to me? I have four feet and you have only two. You haven't got enough shoes for me."

But Little Sambha said, "You could wear them on your ears."

"So I could," said the tiger, "that's a very good idea. Give them to me and I won't eat you this time."

So the tiger got poor Little Sambha's beautiful little purple shoes with crimson soles and crimson linings, and went away saying, "Now I'm the grandest tiger in the jungle."

And by and by Little Sambha met another tiger, and he said to him, "Little Sambha, I'm going to eat you up!" And Little Sambha said, "Oh! Please, Mr. Tiger, don't eat me up, and I'll give you my beautiful green umbrella." But the tiger said, "How can I carry an umbrella when I need all my paws for walking?"

"You could tie a knot on your tail, and carry it that way," said Little Sambha.

"So I could," said the tiger. "Give it to me, and I won't eat you this time."
So the tiger got poor Little Sambha's beautiful green umbrella, and went away saying, "Now I'm the grandest tiger in the jungle." And Little Sambha went away crying because the cruel tigers had taken all his fine clothes.

Presently, he heard a horrible noise that sounded like "Gr-r-r-r-rrr," and it got louder and louder.

"Oh! Dear!" said Little Sambha. "That must be all the tigers coming back to eat me up! What shall I do?" He ran quickly to a palm tree and peeped around it to see what the matter was.

There he saw all the tigers arguing and disputing which of them was the grandest. At last they all got so angry that they knew the only way to settle the argument was to fight. They took off all the fine clothes, so as not to ruin them, and began to tear each other with their claws and bite each other with their great big white teeth.

And they came, rolling and tumbling right to the foot of the very tree where Little Sambha was hiding, but he jumped quickly to hide behind the umbrella.

The tigers all caught hold of each others' tails as they wrangled and scrambled, and so they found themselves in a ring round the tree.

Then, while the tigers were wrangling and scrambling, Little Sambha jumped up, and called out. "Oh, tigers! Why have you taken off all your nice clothes? Don't you want them any more?"

But the tigers only answered, "Gr-r-r!" Then Little Sambha said, "If you want them, say so, or else I'll take them away." But the tigers would not let go of each others' tails and so they could only say, "Grr-r-r-r-r-rrrr!"

39

So Little Sambha put all his fine clothes on again and walked off.

The tigers were very, very angry, but still they would not let go of each others' tails. They were so angry that they ran around the tree trying to eat each other up, and they ran faster and faster until they were whirling round so fast you couldn't see their legs at all.

And they still ran faster and faster and faster until they all just melted away and there was nothing left but a great big pool of melted butter (or *ghi*, as it is called in India) around the base of the tree.

Now Baapa was just coming home from his work with a great big brass pot in his arms and when he saw what was left of all the tigers he said, "Oh! What lovely melted butter! I'll take that home to Maata for her to use in cooking."

So he put it all into the great big brass pot, and took it home to Maata to cook with.

When Maata saw the melted butter, wasn't she pleased! "Now we'll all have pancakes for supper!" she said.

So she got flour and eggs and milk and sugar and butter, and she made a huge big plate of the loveliest pancakes. She fried them in the melted butter that the tigers had made, and they were just as yellow and brown as little tigers.

And then they all sat down to supper.

And Maata ate twenty-seven pancakes.

And Baapa ate fifty-five.

And Little Sambha ate A HUNDRED AND SIXTY-NINE, because he was so hungry.

THE BREMEN
&*Town Musicians*

THERE WAS ONCE A MAN who owned a faithful old donkey that had carried heavy sacks of grain to the mill on its back for many long years. Now that the donkey was old, the poor creature's strength had begun to give out. Seeing this, and knowing that the beast would soon be unfit for work, the man, who was very stingy, began to cut back on the animal's food. The donkey sensed an ill wind was in the air, so one day, when the gate was unlatched, he hit the open road.

"I'll go to Bremen," the donkey said to himself. "I've always wanted to be a musician, and that seems as good a place to start as any!"

As he walked, he came to an old dog that lay stretched out and panting by the side of the road.

"Hello, Hound," said the donkey. "Why so tired? Have you just run a race?"

"You might say that," panted the dog. "I've been racing against time and lost. Ever since my master noticed that I was too old to keep up with the rest of the hunting pack, he's been planning to have me put down. I wasn't about to sit still for that, so I headed out on my own. Now, I don't know which way to turn."

"Hey, I have an idea," said the donkey. "I'm going to Bremen to become a musician. You can come with me and we can make music together. Why, I can play the lute, and you can beat the drum. How about that?"

The dog liked the idea, and the two became a duo of traveling musicians, off to Bremen town.

Before too long, they came upon a cat sitting on the roadside with a face as sad as a week of bad weather.

"Why so glum, old Whiskers?" asked the donkey.

"It's hard to be perky with a noose around your neck," answered the cat gloomily. "Just because I've reached an age where I would rather curl up and purr by the fire than chase mice, my lady wants to stick me in a gunny sack and toss me into the river. I've given her the slip, but now I don't know where my next meal is coming from."

"You can join us!" the donkey suggested. "I'll bet you've sung many a moonlight serenade in your time! Well, we are off to Bremen to become musicians, and could use a cat with your vocal experience!"

And so the duo became a trio of runaway minstrels heading to Bremen town.

Not far down the road they came to a farm, and on the gate sat an old rooster crowing loudly with all his heart and soul.

"Whoa, Chanticleer!" said the donkey. "What are you trying to do, wake the dead?"

"Just a last hurrah," answered the rooster. "I've spent every morning of my life faithfully waking this farmer up so he could start his work day, and what thanks do I get? Tomorrow morning at dawn, the cook is going to throw me into the stew pot for Sunday dinner. Until then, I'm going to cockle-doodle-doo while I've still got the breath to do it!"

"You ought to come with us!" said the donkey. "We are off to Bremen to become musicians. With us, you can sing for your supper rather than become supper!"

The rooster was delighted to join them, and turned the trio into a quartet of fugitive musicians bound for Bremen town.

Bremen town, however, was too far away to be reached in one day, so as evening came on, they found themselves in a forest where they decided to spend the night. The donkey and the dog lay down at the base of a large tree, while the cat and rooster headed up into its branches. The rooster perched at the very top where he felt safest and before going to sleep, he took a last look around them in every direction.

"Hey, down there!" he called to his friends. "I can see a light not far off. It must be a house."

"Let's go!" said the donkey. "The accommodations here aren't exactly great!"

"Sounds good to me," agreed the dog, who thought that wherever there were people there might also be table scraps.

So they set out in the direction of the light, which grew brighter and larger the nearer they got. Soon, in a clearing, they indeed found a well-lit house, but this house was full of robbers who were using it as their den. The donkey, being the tallest, quietly went to the window and peeked in.

"What do you see?" whispered the dog.

"I see a bunch of robbers sitting around a table having a grand old time," he answered quietly. "And no wonder! The table is loaded with all sorts of delicious food and wonderful things to drink!"

"Oh, wouldn't that suit us just fine!" sighed the rooster.

"Yeah," agreed the cat, "but we're out here!"

The animals snuck back into the woods to talk the situation over and at last they had a plan.

The donkey returned to the window and put his front hooves up on a bench that sat beneath it, then the dog jumped onto his back. Quickly, the cat climbed on top of the dog and finally, the rooster flew to his position on the back of the cat.

When everyone was in place, the signal was given and the musicians began to make their music. The donkey brayed, the dog howled, the cat yowled and the rooster crowed. The tuneless uproar burst through the open window in a flood of noise. The robbers, scared out of their wits by the sudden and terrible wail, thought the place was haunted and that ghosts were coming to get them. They ran for their lives into the forest.

The four animals, delighted that their plan was such a success, invited themselves to dinner. Each one found food to his or her liking, and they feasted as if they had been starved for a week. At last they were full and decided to go to bed. The lights were turned out and each one found a suitable place to sleep. The donkey lay down in the yard on a pile of straw near the gate, the dog stretched out by the back door, the cat curled up on the hearth and the rooster flew to the peak of the roof where he perched for the night.

After midnight, the robbers saw, from where they were hiding in the woods, that the house was now dark and all was quiet.

"We shouldn't have been scared off so quickly!" the leader said to the others. "Whatever it was is gone now. You, Shorty," he commanded, "go check the place out and report back to me!"

So the one lone robber crept back into the dark house. Finding nothing but darkness and silence, he made his way to the kitchen. There, in the gloom, he saw what he thought were two glowing embers in the fireplace. In reality what he saw were the shining eyes of the cat.

As the robber knelt near the hearth to light a match by the fiery coals, the cat, who could be very crabby when awoken from a sound sleep, sprang at him, hissing and sputtering and scratching.

Terrified, the robber bolted wildly for the back door, only to be bitten by the dog that was lying there. Dashing out of the house and across the yard, he paused just long enough to open the gate. The donkey then seized the opportunity to give him a good, swift kick with his back hooves as the rooster cried a loud "COCKLE-DOODLE-DOO" from the rooftop.

Tearing through the underbrush and back to his comrades, the robber gave a horrifying account of his adventure in the house. "There is a hideous witch with glowing eyes sitting by the fire that spat at me and scratched my face with her horrible claws. And by the back door lurks a beastlike man who stabbed me with a knife. Then, there was a black monster in the yard that beat me with a wooden club while from the rooftop some goblin judge screamed, "CATCH THAT CROOK, WILL YOU?!!"

None of the other robbers ever set foot in that house again. Whereas the donkey, the dog, the cat and the rooster found it so much to their liking that they lived there happily all the rest of their days.

52

The Three
BILLY GOATS GRUFF

THERE WERE ONCE THREE billy goats who were all brothers and who shared the last name of Gruff. One day, the littlest billy goat decided to go onto the hillside where the grass grew lush and green. There, he thought, he could eat all the delicious grass he wanted. But first he had to go over a bridge that crossed a stream. Trit-trot, trit-trot, the little billy goat's hooves tapped the planks as he made his way across the bridge.

"WHO'S CROSSING MY BRIDGE?" growled the voice of an ugly troll who lived beneath the bridge in its mossy shadows.

"It is only I," bleated a small voice, "the littlest billy goat."

"WELL, LITTLE BILLY GOAT, I'M GOING TO GOBBLE YOU UP!" said the troll.

"Oh, please Mr. Troll," cried the littlest billy goat. "Please don't eat me! I'm so small, I'd barely make a mouthful. But my brother, the second billy goat, who is much bigger and fatter than I am, will be by here soon. Why don't you eat him instead?"

"Oh, alright," the troll grumbled as he settled back onto his slimy rock, "but get off my bridge!"

Much relieved, the littlest billy goat trotted over the bridge and up the hillside, where he immediately began to enjoy the lush, green grass.

Soon, the second billy goat saw his brother grazing happily on the hillside and decided that he too would like to dine there. Trip-trap, trip-trap, the second billy goat's hooves sounded on the planks of the old bridge.

"WHO'S CROSSING MY BRIDGE?!" growled the troll from beneath those planks.

"It is only I," said a medium-sized voice, "the second billy goat."

"WELL, SECOND BILLY GOAT, I'M GOING TO GOBBLE YOU UP!" said the troll.

"Oh, please Mr. Troll," cried the goat. "Please don't eat me! I wouldn't make much of a meal compared to my big brother, the biggest billy goat. He's much bigger and fatter than I am. Why don't you eat him instead when he comes by?"

"Oh, alright," grumbled the Troll, who was getting hungrier and crabbier, "but get the heck off my bridge!"

So, with a sigh of relief, the second billy goat hurried over the bridge and up the hillside where he and his little brother together enjoyed the lush, green grass.

Soon, the biggest billy goat noticed that his little brothers were getting fat on the hillside and he decided to join them. CLIP-CLOP, CLIP-CLOP, the biggest billy goat's hooves sounded loudly as he walked across the bridge and the planks bent under his weight.

"WHO IS CROSSING MY BRIDGE?!!" growled the hungry troll.

"IT IS I," growled a large voice in return, "I AM THE BIGGEST BILLY GOAT! WHO ARE YOU?"

"I AM THE TROLL!" came a snarling reply. "AND THIS IS MY BRIDGE YOU ARE CLOMPING OVER! SO NOW, BIGGEST BILLY GOAT, I'M GOING TO GOBBLE YOU UP!" and with that the great drooling troll came climbing up over the edge of the bridge.

Without another word, the biggest billy goat lowered his head, positioned his horns and charged, full force, into the oncoming troll.

There was a loud SPLASH as the troll fell into the river. Instantly, the swift current carried him downstream, around the bend and out of sight. The biggest billy goat snorted, and then casually strolled across the bridge and up the hillside. There, he joined his brothers and, if they are not gone, then they are there still, enjoying the lush, green grass.

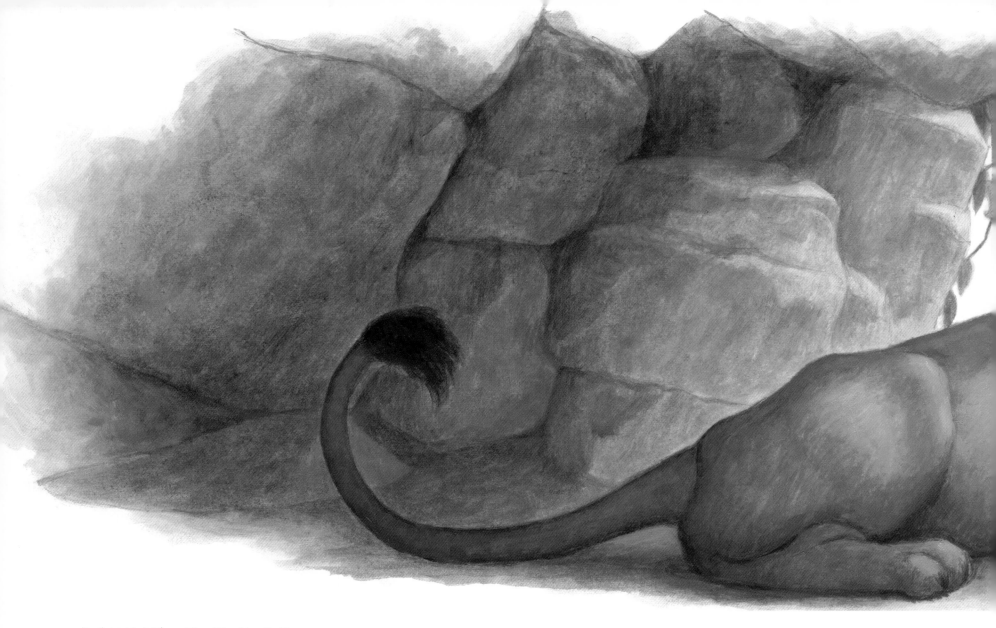

THE LION
and the Mouse

ONE MORNING, a lion, who was asleep in his den, was awakened by a playful mouse running across his face. In an instant, the giant cat had the little rodent pinned to the floor of the cave. Within his huge paw, the lion could feel the tiny creature's heart racing inside its chest.

"Please don't eat me!" cried the terrified mouse. "If you spare me, I promise, somehow, some way, to repay your kindness!"

"HA, HA!" the lion's great laugh echoed through the cave. "To think some-one your size could somehow help me. HA!"

"Well," the lion continued, "you do have a sense of humor, I'll grant you that." The lion was mighty but he wasn't cruel, so he opened his paw and the mouse scampered away.

"Thank you!" a little voice squeaked from the mouth of the cave, "and remember, I'll be around if you need me!"

The lion snorted a "Yeah, OK. Any time!" under his breath, chuckled, then rolled over and went back to sleep.

One day, not long after this, the lion happened to find himself trapped in a net set in the jungle by poachers. He tore and fought against the ropes but even his powerful teeth and claws were no match for the net. The more he fought, the more tightly the knotted cords held him in their grasp. Finally, the struggle exhausted the lion and with his heart pounding, he roared in angry frustration.

Suddenly, a familiar squeak reached the helpless lion. "I thought that was you!" he said.

Pinned beneath the net, the lion felt the feet of the little mouse scamper across his face.

"Now, I'd say this job calls for someone just about my size!" The mouse winked at the lion and began to gnaw the rope with his sharp, little teeth. Within minutes, the ropes were chewed right through and all the animals of the jungle heard the mighty lion's thankful roar.

But only a few were close enough to hear the reply of the tiny mouse: "Any time!"

JACK AND THE
Beanstalk

ONCE UPON A TIME, a widow and her son, Jack, lived in a cottage at the edge of a forest. They were very poor and Jack, who was a bright lad, could have been more helpful to his mother but because she expected little of him, little is what she got. They were so poor that all they had to live on was the milk from their faithful old cow, Bossie. But then the day came when Bossie could give no more milk.

"Now what?" cried the poor woman. "Without that milk we shall surely starve!"

"I guess the only thing left to do is for me to take Bossie to the market and see if I can sell her," said Jack.

Jack's mother disagreed. She knew the boy had never bartered in the market-place before, and she feared he'd be unable to get a good price. Jack knew, however, that they had no other choice and soon she agreed to let him go.

"Just make sure you get a good price, Jack!" she called after him as he led the cow towards town. "She's all we have!"

Jack hadn't traveled very far when he came upon a peddler resting by the roadside. The man asked the boy where he was bound with the old cow. When Jack explained he was off to the market to fetch the best price he could for her, the peddler smiled. He pulled a small bag from his pocket and said, "I have the best price right here, laddie, beans, magic beans!"

"Beans for a cow?" Jack laughed, but as he turned to go, the peddler poured the beans from the bag into his other hand. They were large, polished smooth, and richly colored.

"Magic beans..." the peddler smiled and held them out to Jack. Something about those beans caught his eye and drew him closer, and he wanted them more than he had ever wanted any other thing in his whole life. Within moments, the trade was made and Jack was walking away clutching the bag of beans.

"Be careful, Jack," the peddler called after him. "Remember, those aren't just any old beans. Those are magic beans!"

But the boy didn't hear him. He was already hurrying home, eager to show his mother the good bargain that he had made.

"YOU WHAT?!" the poor woman sobbed as Jack repeated once more that he had traded their cow for a handful of beans.

"But they're magic," Jack said, offering them to her in his outstretched hand.

"Ohhh!" she cried in disgust. "Get those things away from me!" As she slapped his hand away, the beans flew through the open window and out into the garden.

Feeling foolish and ashamed, Jack went to bed that night without any supper. As usual, he was awakened early the next morning by his growling stomach, but this morning was different. His bedroom was unusually dark. Something big had grown up overnight outside his window, and was now blocking the sunlight.

"It's the beans!" Jack exclaimed, and he raced outside into the garden. There, he found a huge bean plant as big around as a tree trunk, twisting up out of the flowerbed. It grew like a winding ladder, higher than their cottage and higher than the treetops, up and up, until it disappeared into the clouds.

In a twinkling, Jack began climbing the giant beanstalk. Hand over hand he climbed, scrambling higher and higher into the sky. He climbed all that

day until, at last, he found himself in the clouds. He was tired but pressed on, hoping to see what lay ahead. He emerged from the cloud bank to find that he had reached the beanstalk's end. All around him, as far as he could see, rocks and hills seemed to float in a sea of clouds. Far in the distance, a castle rose out of the mist. Suddenly, Jack's stomach grumbled to remind him of just how empty it was. Hoping he might beg a meal at the castle, he leapt to a nearby rock and struck out for the distant palace.

When at last Jack came to the castle steps, he had to stretch on tiptoe to reach a huge, rusty knocker that hung from the heavy door. He could barely lift it before letting it fall, and a loud clang followed that echoed through the halls within. Soon, the door opened and a very tall woman squinted down at him.

"My eyes aren't what they used to be," she said, "but you're not from around here, are you?"

Jack shook his head.

"I didn't think so, because my husband is a horrible ogre who has eaten every human being for fifty miles," she said, "so you better scat if you know what's good for you."

"If only I could, Ma'am," Jack feebly replied, "but I'm so tired and hungry I'm afraid I'm going to faint." And with that, the poor boy's knees buckled and he began to sink onto the steps.

"Oh, all right," she said, taking pity on him. "You can come in, but just long enough to eat a bowl of porridge. My husband is due home any time now, and if he catches you here it will be the devil to pay for both of us!"

The ogre's wife led Jack down a winding stone corridor and into a large kitchen. A huge, black cauldron full of porridge simmered over the fire. The woman told Jack to sit down on the hearth while she filled a bowl for him. This she gave him, along with a hunk of fresh bread and a cupful of milk.

Food had never tasted so good, and Jack ate heartily, despite the strange surroundings. Just as he finished the last bite, thunderous sounds shook the castle walls.

"That's my husband!" the woman gasped. "Quick! The cupboard!" she cried, and as Jack leapt into the cabinet she closed the door behind him, then tossed his bowl, cup and spoon into the soapy water in the dish tub.

Luckily, the cupboard door didn't close completely, so Jack held his breath and peeked out.

A second later, the biggest two-legged creature the boy had ever seen lumbered into the kitchen. The giant threw a huge wooden club and a cloth sack, bulging with stolen booty, into the corner. Then, he turned and sniffed the air.

"Fee, Fie, Fo, Fum. I smell the blood of an Englishman!" he roared.

"Bah," said his wife, waving her hand. "You're always smelling things. Why, you probably stepped in something. Did you wipe your feet?" she asked, pointing to his big, dirty shoes.

The ogre gave a defiant snort, but then looked first at the bottom of one shoe and then the other.

"Well," he grumbled, as he flopped into a huge chair, "I did smell something…"

Immediately, the woman began placing food on the table before her ogre-of-a-husband. Amazed, Jack watched as the giant devoured bowlful after bowlful of steaming porridge, never stopping until the huge cauldron was empty and every one of the heaping plates was bare. As the poor woman began to clear away the dirty dishes, the ogre roared, "Wife, fetch my hen!"

Soon, a pretty hen was strutting around the tabletop and as the ogre stroked her soft feathers, she clucked and cooed with delight.

"Now, my pretty hen, lay me an egg!" the ogre commanded, and sure enough, after a few squawks and clucks, the hen produced an egg, a beautiful golden egg. Even though the giant laughed with glee, his guffaws soon turned to yawns, and his head began to nod. Before long, he was snoring in his chair.

When Jack realized that the giant was asleep, he wasted no time in creeping quietly from his hiding place. As he tiptoed past the table and heard the ogre's snores and the hen's soft clucking, the temptation was just too much.

Within seconds, Jack climbed onto the table and quickly, but gently, grabbed the hen. A moment later, he was running down the stone corridor and as the big castle door closed behind him, the ogre's snores faded and Jack disappeared into the night.

It was nearly daybreak when Jack and the hen reached the top of the beanstalk. Fearful that the ogre would awaken and discover his missing pet, Jack dared not slow his pace, and he scurried down as fast as he could. He never paused, not even when invited to breakfast by a friendly crow and hungry squirrel, who were preparing to dine on one of the stalk's giant green beans.

By mid-morning, Jack was presenting his mother with his wonderful prize. She was delighted, and for months they lived very well on the money they made selling the little hen's golden eggs. Even so, Jack couldn't help thinking about another adventure on the beanstalk. When he told his mother his thoughts, she discouraged him. Why should he go looking for trouble, especially now that they had this wonderful hen?

Then, one day, the hen didn't lay her usual egg, and one day became two days and then three. Frightened that the golden eggs could stop the same way Bossie's milk had, Jack's mother soon changed her mind and the next morning the boy was making another climb up the beanstalk.

For weeks, Jack had been thinking about a return visit to the ogre's castle. He remembered that his wife had poor eyesight so Jack hoped that if he wore a disguise and changed his voice she might not recognize him. So once again, after making his way to the front door of the castle, he lifted the heavy knocker, and once again the ogre's wife stood squinting down at him.

"Haven't I seen you before?" she asked.

"I don't believe I've had the pleasure of being introduced, Madam," the boy answered in a deep voice as he bowed slightly and smiled. "My name is Jack."

"Hmmm, maybe not…" she said, sizing him up. "That other little beggar was smaller and scrawnier, I think."

"I am no beggar, Madame," said Jack, "but just a weary traveler who would appreciate a place to rest and perhaps a crust of bread."

"Well," said the woman, taking pity on him, "maybe just a crust of bread." Opening the door wider she let Jack in. "But beware! My husband is an ogre, and if he catches you here, you'll find yourself roasting over the kitchen fire. And mind, you'd better not steal from him like that last little thief!"

Jack nodded and followed her into the kitchen. All was as it had been before, except this time it was a hearty stew that simmered in the cauldron. The woman gave him a bowlful, and then continued her dinner preparations. Once again, Jack had just finished his last bit of food when the thunderous arrival of the ogre was heard.

This time, however, the woman pointed Jack to the oven, where he climbed inside and hid. No sooner had this been done, than the ogre stormed into the room. As with the cupboard, this new hiding place gave Jack a great view. He could peek out through a gap in the oven door.

"Fee, Fie, Fo, Fum! I smell the blood of an Englishman!" roared the ogre.

"There you go again!" said his wife. "That's the third time this week you've smelled something. Well, I've just spent the whole day cleaning," she pointed to a mop and buckets in the corner, "so don't go blaming me! It's probably that cheese in the pantry."

"Cheese, my eye…" the ogre grumbled, as he threw himself into his chair and snorted.

Immediately, his wife placed a tub-sized bowl of hot stew before him. The ogre seemed to forget all else as he devoured every particle of food that came into his sight. The woman continued serving him stew by the tubful, until the ogre finally declared himself stuffed.

"Wife!" he commanded loudly as she cleared the table. "Fetch me my gold!"

Grumbling, she struggled to bring in three bags of gold, and once they were placed upon the table, she was ordered from the room. You see, the ogre trusted no one, not even his wife, for the giant had stolen this gold and he feared others might do the same to him. Once he was alone, he counted each and every coin until the tabletop surrounding him was a wall of golden stacks.

Then, he carefully returned each coin to the bag from which it had come. By the time he'd replaced the last coin in the last bag, he began to nod and yawn, and soon his great head was down on the table, and the sound of his monstrous snoring filled the room.

Within minutes, Jack had slipped from the oven and was up on the table. Holding his breath, the boy gingerly leaned over a huge hand. All the while, the giant's foul snorting breath ruffled Jack's hair. Though he wanted more, the smallest bag was all he could carry. It was a challenge getting down off the table without making a sound, but Jack managed it. Once, some of the coins clinked and the snoring stopped suddenly, but by the time it resumed, Jack was closing the heavy castle door behind himself as he headed back to the beanstalk.

Jack's mother was overjoyed with the bag of gold. At last, she thought, their troubles were over. This treasure would take care of everything. And so it did, at least for a while. They lived well for months and were very generous with relatives and friends, but alas, even the biggest bag of gold has a last coin in it somewhere.

And yet, that was all right with Jack. The beanstalk, after all, was just outside his window and never far from his thoughts. The next climb was always on his mind.

Early one morning, wearing yet another disguise, Jack set out once again. As he climbed, he practiced talking to himself in funny voices, trying to find one that would fool the ogre's wife just one more time. It didn't seem long before he was standing at the ogre's door, preparing to knock.

"Hola, Frauline," said Jack, as the woman opened the heavy door. "Me come from very long way," he continued in his best foreign accent. "Much hungry!"

"A foreigner, aye?" the woman squinted at him as before. "You do look odd!"

"Please," said Jack in a high, weak voice, "just a leetle beet of food, pretty lady?"

"Very well," she said, "but just a morsel, then out you go. My husband, the ogre, will cook us both for supper if he finds out that I let a stranger in after his gold was stolen."

Everything was as it had been before, except soup was for dinner this evening. Almost like clockwork, as Jack slurped his last spoonful of broth, the castle shook with the ogre's return.

The woman practically threw Jack into a large copper pot that stood on the shelf. In her haste to put the cover on, she left the lid slightly askew and Jack peeked out to see her bustling away.

"Fee, Fie, Fo, Fum. I smell the blood of an Englishman!" The ogre's loud voice made Jack's kettle ring.

"Englishman?" laughed his wife. "All I smell is that skunk that's made a nest in the woodpile. Englishman, indeed!"

But before the ogre could growl another word, she ladled a gallon of the steaming soup into his bowl. The food did the trick and with his mind completely occupied, the ogre's tiny brain had little room for other thoughts. He slurped contentedly away, at least for as long as the soup lasted.

"Now, wife!" said the ogre, wiping his soup-stained hands on his shirt. "Take these empty bowls away and fetch my harp!"

All was done as commanded, and soon the most beautiful golden harp that Jack had ever seen sat glistening before the ogre.

"Play, harp!" ordered the ogre. "Play!"

To Jack's amazement, the harp began to play a haunting melody. But that was not the only tune that it knew, for throughout the course of the evening the instrument favored the ogre with lively jigs, lovely airs and beautiful ballads. As Jack listened, he imagined himself and the harp touring the world, performing for audiences in foreign lands. He knew then that he must have this magic harp.

It was during a lullaby that the ogre drifted off to sleep and his familiar snoring began. Jack was out of the pot and down off the shelf within moments. He made it silently across the table, seized the harp and then he got a terrible surprise.

"Master, Master!" the harp cried. The harp could not only play music, but it could also speak, and Jack had startled it. Still clutching the magic harp, Jack darted across the tabletop, but this time the ogre was awake.

"STOP, THIEF!" he roared, lunging for the boy.

With surprising speed, a huge hand shot towards him. Fortunately, Jack was just beyond its reach. Leaping from table to chair to floor, he was racing down the stone corridor in no time. Behind him, he could hear the raging ogre upend his chair and overturn the table as he reached for his club in the corner. When Jack raced out the front door, the thundering footfalls of the ogre followed him. Luckily for the boy, the ogre was old and full of soup, and not as fast as he might have been.

Reaching the stalk, Jack peered back through the mist to see the ogre's towering form, club in hand, running towards him. Grasping the harp, Jack leapt and jumped down the beanstalk for all he was worth.

As soon as their cottage came into view he called out.

"MOTHER! QUICK! THE AXE!"

As he leaped to the ground, she was there waiting, and with all the breath he had left in him he swung the axe. CHOP! CHOP! CHOP! He could see the ogre's legs coming down the stalk above him.

CHOP! CHOP! The beanstalk started to sway.

CHOP! With one last blow the towering beanstalk cracked, gave a mighty groan, then fell, crashing into the forest. The earth shook as somewhere deep in the woods the falling ogre met his doom.

In time, the magic harp did change Jack's life, though not quite in the way he had imagined when he first saw it. They did, indeed, set out to tour the world, and Jack hoped the harp would make his fortune as people flocked to hear it play, but he and the harp made it only as far as the neighboring kingdom.

There, during a command performance for the King and his beautiful young daughter, the Princess became enchanted by more than just the harp.

Years later, after Jack and the Princess were married and Jack's mother was generously taken care of, he would sometimes pause at a palace window. And there, looking out across the rolling lands over which he and the Princess ruled, he couldn't help but smile to himself as he remembered that all of this had started with a handful of beans, magic beans!

A Note from the Artist

In many ways, this book has been years in the making. Not only does my love for these stories go back to my own childhood, but as an adult, I have wanted to illustrate them for decades. The picture of Jack coming down the beanstalk, for example, was actually painted back in 1991, and my serious interest in illustrating a tale which, for this collection is entitled "The Story of Little Sambha and the Tigers," began several years after that. Originally called "The Story of Little Black Sambo," it was written in 1899 by Helen Bannerman. In 1994, I had a conversation with a grammar school teacher about favorite old stories that would make great picture books and "Little Black Sambo" came up. We both agreed that it was too bad that so many of the old illustrated versions had depicted the boy and his parents as caricatures of Black stereotypes, spoiling an otherwise charming story.

"It's interesting that the author wrote it as a story about a boy in India," the teacher said. I hadn't heard that before, so on my next visit to the library I did some research and she was right. Mrs. Bannerman was born in Scotland, but had lived in India for thirty years. Suddenly, the Indian connection seemed obvious in the story as well, for not only did it feature tigers (native to India) but it also used the word "ghi" which the author tells us is the Indian word for melted butter. I thought, why not illustrate the story with an Indian family? I was excited about reintroducing this great old tale in a new light but, other work commitments forced me to add this to my ever-growing wish list.

Fast-forward sixteen years, and I began a collection of classic bedtime stories. I dusted off my wish list and thought that not only would this be a perfect opportunity to fully illustrate several stories like "Jack and the Beanstalk," for which I had done only a single painting earlier, but perhaps the time had finally come for me to try my hand at that other old favorite. Indian names were given to the boy and his parents, and soon "The Story of Little Sambha and the Tigers" joined the collection. I never would have predicted the decades-long arc this project would take, but I was right about one thing; it was an awful lot of fun to do. As far as what readers may think of my interpretation of these stories, I guess only time will tell, but I hope they will enjoy them as much I have.